THE OWL AND THE PUSSYCAT

—a parody

BRIAN WILSON

Other books by Brian Wilson

SHORT STORIES

Moments in Time

A collection of short stories, 2012

Bumpy Roads

A collection of short stories, 2013

Here Comes the Sun-Perhaps?

A collection of short stories, 2015

So that's Life?

A collection of short stories, 2016

NOVELS

Operation Iran, 2016

The First Trumpet, 2017

Treasure of the General Grant, 2020

CHILDREN'S BOOKS

It was the night before Christmas, 2020

ABOUT THE AUTHOR

Brian Wilson is a New Zealand writer of novels, short stories and children's books. He has an MA(hon) in psychology and is married with three adult children and eight grandchildren.

Website: https://www.brian-d-wilson.com/

ISBN: 9780473588571

DEDICATION

To my grandchildren

The Owl and the Pussycat- A parody

The Owl and the Pussy cat were out at sea

Trapped in a ship's life-raft

The pussy found rations enough for tea

Tucked away in the small boat's aft.

The owl searched longingly for land all day

While singing to please the cat,

My lovely pussy and sweet they say

And a beautiful pussy at that,

At that

At that

And a beautiful pussy at that.

Said Pussy to the Owl, while licking his lip,

"How charmingly sweet you smell!

You're the heavenly part to this unplanned trip

Come closer so more I can tell."

But sadly to the cat's dismay

Owl remained perched on the mast

While they continued drifting for many a day.

Pussy would have to fast

To fast

To fast

Pussy would have to fast

“I’m very hungry.”

Owl flapped her wings to prepare for flight

"Oh you're such a beautiful fowl,"

Said Pussy as she relished the sight

"My beautiful, beautiful owl."

"Now I'm even more hungry."

“We could get married, you’re such a prize.

Come down and do what’s right.”

“Sorry my Pussy I am to wise”

And at that the owl took flight

Took flight,

Took flight,

And at that the owl took flight.

To the land where the Bongo-Tree grows she flew

Where she found a safe new home.

Pussy Cat later arrived there too

And found he was not alone.

Haha, safe at last.

Food in abundance to see him well

Including mice to his nice surprise

But nothing was as tempting as that beautiful owl

Gone, because she was too wise,

Too wise,

Too wise,

Gone, because she was too wise.

Brian Wilson

CPSIA information can be obtained
at www.ICGtesting.com
Printed in the USA
LVHW070342061021
699649LV00006B/316

9 780473 588571